This book belong

Music +
movement

Published by Scholastic Inc., 90 Old Sherman Turnpike, Danbury, CT 06816

SCHOLASTIC and associated logos are trademarks and/or registered trademarks of Scholastic Inc.

ISBN 0-439-90702-0

Printed in the U.S.A.

First Scholastic Printing, December 2006

Tappety-Tap, Swish, Strum

by
Sarah Albee

illustrated by
Dave Aikins

SCHOLASTIC INC.

New York   Toronto   London   Auckland   Sydney
Mexico City   New Delhi   Hong Kong   Buenos Aires

Once upon a time, there was a kingdom without music. No one had ever tried to play music.

No one
had ever even *heard*
music! The only sounds were
the noises of the townspeople,
doing their jobs.

7

Cobbler Tyrone made shoes. Tap-tap-tappety-tap went his little hammer.

Farmer Austin cut his wheat. Swish-swish! went his thresher.

Milkmaid Uniqua carried her buckets to market. Squeak-squeak went the handles.

Shepherd Pablo took his sheep to pasture. Clip-clop, clip-clop was the sound their hooves made.

Princess Tasha lived in a castle on a hill high above the town. Every afternoon, the princess lay down for her royal nap. But she always had trouble falling asleep.

She tossed and turned. She put her velvet pillows over her head.

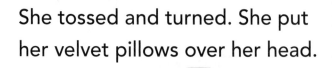

She tried reading stories.
She tried drinking warm milk.

She even tried counting Shepherd Pablo's sheep as they passed below her window. Clip-clop, clip-clop went their hooves.

"What could be keeping me up?" asked the princess, drumming her fingers on her royal windowsill.

Just then Princess Tasha became aware of all the noises coming from the town.

Tap-tap-tappety-tap went the hammer.

Swish-swish went the thresher.

Clip-clop, clip-clop went the sheep's hooves.

Squeak-squeak went the bucket handles.

"Hey, Villagers!" the princess shouted down from her turret window. "You're keeping me awake with all your noises! I command everyone to be quiet from now on!"

So the people of the town tried to work more quietly.
They stopped tapping, swishing, clip-clopping, and
squeaking. They tiptoed to and fro, so they would not
disturb the princess.

The very next day, Princess Tasha settled down for her royal nap. She listened for noises, but all was quiet. "Now that's more like it!" she said as she patted her royal pillow.

Over in the cobbler's shop, Cobbler Tyrone was trying to work quietly, but then he accidentally twanged a boot lace. "What a cool sound!" he whispered to himself. And he began to strum.

Strum, strum, strum.

With his other hand, he tapped his hammer on the sole of the boot.

Tippety-tap, tippety tap.

"Hey, nice sound!" called Shepherd Pablo from his pasture.
He picked a blade of grass and began tooting on it.

Strum, strum. Tippety-tap, tippety tap. Toot! Toot! The two began to walk along, playing their cheerful sounds. They passed Farmer Austin planting seeds in his fields. He looked up and gave his packet of seeds a little shake.

Shakey-shakey-shakey-shakey went his packet of seeds.
The seed sounds added a jazzy beat. He dropped his hoe
and joined the others as they marched.

Milkmaid Uniqua was so enchanted by the sounds that she overturned an empty bucket and began to drum on it. Then she fell into step behind the others.

Plunkety-plunk! went the bucket.

Down the lane went
the marchers.
Strum, strum. Tippety, tap. Thunk.
Shakey-shakey-shakey-shakey,
Toot! Toot! PLUNK!
So amazed were the
marchers to be playing
music, they did not realize
how much noise
they were making.

Back in the palace, Princess Tasha was trying to get to sleep.

"Now it's too quiet!" she grumbled. "How is a princess supposed to sleep when the whole kingdom is so quiet?"

Then she heard a sound she had never heard before. She went to the window.

"Hey! Is that you guys making those sounds?" he called down to the marchers.

"Uh-oh," gulped Shepherd Pablo.

"Yeah. Uh-oh," agreed Cobbler Tyrone.

"Yes, your Highness," Farmer Austin admitted.

"We're sorry if we disturbed your nap," added Milkmaid Uniqua.

23

"Never mind my nap!" said the delighted princess.
"I command you to keep playing! I'll be right down!"

The surprised marchers looked at one another. They began to play their lovely new music again. A moment later, the princess joined the group, pinging a silver spoon against her royal milk bottle.

Ping-ping-ping!
went the spoon.
   The group of musicians began to march down the street in time to their cheerful music.

And from that day forward, there was always music in the kingdom!

Nick Jr. Play-to-Learn™ Fundamentals

Skills every child needs, in stories every child will love!

colors + shapes
Recognizing and identifying basic shapes and colors in the context of a story.

emotions
Learning to identify and understand a wide range of emotions: happy, sad, excited, frustrated, etc.

imagination
Fostering creative thinking skills through role-play and make-believe.

math
Recognizing early math in the world around us: patterns, shapes, numbers, sequences.

music + movement
Celebrating the sounds and rhythms of music and dance.

physical
Building coordination and confidence through physical activity and play.

problem solving
Using critical thinking skills (observing, listening, following directions) to make predictions and solve problems.

reading + language
Developing a lifelong love of reading through high interest stories and characters.

science
Fostering curiosity and an interest in the natural world around us.

social skills + cultural diversity
Developing respect for others as unique, interesting people.

Conversation Spark

Questions and activities for play–to–learn parenting.

Join the band! Find objects in your house or outside, just like the Backyardigans. Make your own homemade instruments, then play away!

For more parent and kid-friendly activities, go to www.nickjr.com.